Alexander McCall Smith

Teacher Trouble

ILLUSTRATED BY
JON RILEY

YOUNG CORGI BOOKS

TEACHER TROUBLE
A YOUNG CORGI BOOK 0 552 52803 X

First published in Great Britain by Young Corgi Books

PRINTING HISTORY
Young Corgi edition published 1994
Reprinted 1994 (twice), 1995 (three times)

Text copyright © 1994 by Alexander McCall-Smith
Illustrations copyright © 1994 by Jon Riley
Cover artwork by Nick Sharratt

Set in 14/18 Linotype Garamond by Chippendale Type Ltd, Otley, West Yorkshire

Young Corgi Books are published by Transworld Publishers Ltd, 61–63 Uxbridge Road, Ealing, London W5 5SA, in Australia by Transworld Publishers (Australia) Pty Ltd, 15–25 Helles Avenue, Moorebank, NSW 2170, and in New Zealand by Transworld Publishers (NZ) Ltd, 3 William Pickering Drive, Albany, Auckland.

Reproduced, printed and bound in Great Britain by Cox & Wyman Ltd, Reading, Berkshire

This book is for my godson,
James Fitzroy Bruce Maclean

CONTENTS

Chapter One

Jenny was very tall. She had always been tall, right from the very beginning, and now that she was ten she was almost as tall as most grown-ups, and a good deal taller than some. This was often very useful. She always came first at high jump, and in libraries she was able to reach books from the shelves that nobody else could reach. The best books were always to be found there, she thought.

But there were times when it was

certainly a bit of a nuisance being tall. It was sometimes quite difficult to get clothes that were just the right size, and the desks at school often didn't have quite enough knee-room. And then there were occasions when being tall led to quite remarkable things, as happened with the great mistake.

It all started when Jenny had to change schools. Her family had moved to a new town and Jenny and her brother had to go to new schools. Her brother was older than she was, and so he was to go to one school while she was to go to another. Jenny, in fact, had a choice of two schools.

The schools wrote to her mother and sent their brochures. Each had a picture on the front page and inside you could read about what the schools were like. There was nothing particularly unusual about these schools, but there was a very curious thing about their names.

One was called the Pond Street School and the other was called Street Pond School. This was very strange, as they were not far from one another and Jenny thought that it must have led to lots of mix-ups.

And she was right. There had been lots of confusion. For example, the mail for the Principal of Street Pond School often went to the Principal of Pond Street School, and the other way round. Sometimes Pond Street School got a bill which was meant for Street Pond School – and paid it – which meant that when the mistake was discovered, Street Pond School had to pay Pond Street School back.

Sometimes Street Pond School won a competition, but the papers announced that Pond Street School had won. This made Street Pond School furious, and there would have to be an announcement in the papers that Pond

Street School hadn't won anything at all, which made Pond Street School furious – because they sometimes won things anyway. So it was all very confusing.

Jenny could not make up her mind which school she preferred, and so her mother chose for her and Jenny agreed with the choice.

"Pond Street School looks fine," said her mother. "I think you should go to that one."

Jenny agreed. The name sounded quite nice and she was sure that she would make new friends there.

On her first morning at the new school, Jenny got everything ready in good time. She packed her bag with the new pencil case she had bought and with all the other things that she was bound to need. Her mother had insisted that she dress as smartly as she could on her first day at school, and had made her wear a dress which Jenny didn't really like.

"It's such an old-fashioned dress," Jenny complained. "It makes me look so old."

"Nonsense," her mother retorted. "You can't go to your new school wearing jeans and a scruffy T-shirt. You look very good in that dress."

Jenny knew that it was no good arguing with her mother when she had made up her mind about something. So she put on the old-fashioned dress and went down to breakfast. Then, when she was finally ready to leave the house, her father and mother both wished her good luck.

"I'll drive you to school," her father offered.

"No thank you," said Jenny. "I know the way . . . I think."

Jenny waved to her parents and began the short walk that would lead her to the front gate of her new school. She felt

very excited, and a bit anxious, as you always do when you are about to start a new school and aren't quite sure what everybody will be like. She wondered whether she would meet many new friends there. She had had very good friends at her last school and she had been sorry to leave them. She hoped that the pupils at her new school would be as nice, or at least almost as nice.

As she drew near to the new school she began to walk more slowly. It was far bigger than her last school, she thought, and there were many more pupils milling about. And where was she meant to go? Should she walk straight in the main entrance and try to find the office, or should she look for some children who were about her age and just follow them in? She could always ask somebody to help her, of course, but she didn't know anybody and everyone except her seemed to be busy talking to their friends.

Jenny arrived at the entrance to the school and looked about her. Nobody was taking any notice of her and so she decided just to stand there for a little while and see what happened. Perhaps one of the teachers would come and ask her her name and then take her to her classroom.

"Good morning."

Jenny spun round. One of the teachers had come up and was standing right behind her. Jenny noticed that she was taller than the teacher, who was smiling at her in a friendly manner.

"So there you are," said the teacher. "We've been expecting you."

"Oh, good," said Jenny. She was pleased to hear that they knew she was coming. This meant that she wouldn't have to ask her way after all.

"If you'd like to come along with me," said the teacher, "I'll show you where your classroom is."

Jenny followed as the teacher led the way. They went into the building and walked along a long corridor past the open doors of several classrooms. Jenny noticed that most of the classrooms had now filled up with pupils and that lessons were just about to begin.

"By the way," said the teacher. "I

didn't introduce myself. My name is Alison."

Jenny was rather surprised. Alison sounded like a first name, and it was rather odd for a teacher to give her first name to a pupil. Perhaps this was a very friendly school, where everybody called the teachers Mary, and John, or whatever their first names might be. Jenny had heard about schools like that before, but she had never actually been in one.

They stopped outside the door of the last classroom in the corridor.

"Here we are," said the teacher. "This is your classroom."

Jenny looked through the door. The classroom was full, and all the pupils were seated at their desks, looking at her. She wished that she had arrived earlier. Nobody would have paid so much attention to her if she had arrived at the same time as everybody else.

They went into the classroom and everybody stopped talking.

"Good morning class," said the teacher.

As the class replied, Jenny glanced nervously about the room. She was surprised to see that everybody looked younger than she did – at least one or two years younger. But perhaps I am imagining it, she thought. Perhaps it's

just because I'm not used to them.

She looked around the room again. Every single desk was occupied and there did not appear to be a single seat left. She looked at the teacher.

"Excuse me," she said. "Where do I sit?"

The teacher looked at her in surprise, and then smiled.

"Yes," she said. "I'm sorry. The school is a bit crowded. But don't

worry, we've kept your seat free."

And with that she pointed to the chair behind the table facing the class. The teacher's seat!

Chapter Two

For a moment, Jenny did not know what to think. The teacher had definitely pointed to that chair, and her ears had not been deceiving her when she heard her tell her that she was to sit there. But where was the teacher going to sit herself? Would she walk about the classroom or just stand in the same place all day? Surely she would need to sit down some time.

"Well," said the teacher. "I'll leave you to get on with it. I've got to go and teach my class. But I'll come back when the break bell goes and show you where the staff room is."

Staff room? Why should I need to know where the staff room is? Jenny asked herself. Perhaps I might have to run an errand for a teacher some time. But there was still the problem of the chair. Perhaps she should do as she was told and sit in it after all.

Jenny went towards the teacher's chair and sat in it, feeling very embarrassed as she did so. Yet although everybody was staring at her, nobody was laughing.

"By the way," said the teacher as she left the room. "You'll find the register in the top drawer of the desk. The Principal likes it to be called first thing every morning."

Jenny was astonished. Usually teachers called the register, but perhaps this school was different. Well, if that's

STREET POND SCHOOL

REGISTER

CLASS... Mrs B...

what they wanted her to do, she could do it for them . . .

The teacher now left the classroom and Jenny opened the top drawer of the desk. There was a large brown book, which she took out and opened at the first page. There was a list of names, written out in alphabetical order, and against them neat lines of ticks and crosses had been put in.

Everybody was quiet as Jenny called out the first name.

"George Apple," she called.

"Yes," said a boy from the front row. "Yes, I'm here."

Jenny put a tick after George Apple's name.

"Caroline Box," she called.

There was no reply, so Jenny called out the name again in case Caroline Box had not heard.

Still there was no reply. Then a girl sitting at the front put up her hand.

"Please, miss," she said. "Caroline Box isn't well. She lives next door to me and her mother said she had a bad cold."

"Oh, I see," said Jenny, putting a cross against the name. Then she stopped, her hand frozen where it was. The girl had called her "miss"! Why on earth should she do that. It was not as if she was a teacher.

Suddenly, and with a terrible bump, it

26

all fell into place. No! Surely the teacher couldn't have mistaken her . . . for a teacher! It was quite impossible. And yet, everything seemed to point to this. She had been shown the teacher's chair. She had been told about the staff room. She had been asked to call the register.

Jenny's mind raced as she thought about the terrible mistake that had been made. She was tall, of course, and people often said she could be mistaken for a grown-up. But nobody had ever actually made that mistake, and certainly nobody had ever mistaken her for a teacher!

They must have been expecting a new teacher, she thought. Then, when they saw me standing at the gate, they must have thought that I was the person they were waiting for. It was an awful mistake to have been made, but it had been made and here she was in charge of a whole class, calling the register! The very thought made Jenny's skin come out in goose-bumps. It was the most embarrassing, terrible thing that had ever happened to her. It was a complete and utter nightmare.

Without really thinking of what she was doing, Jenny continued to call the register. Then, when all the names had been called, she replaced the book in the drawer of the desk and took a deep breath. The simplest thing to do would be to get to her feet and to rush out of the room. She would run out of the school and all the way home and tell her parents all about the terrible mistake.

She looked at the people in front of her. They were all sitting quite still, waiting for her to begin. Somehow it seemed impossible to rise to her feet and run out of the room. Her legs just would not carry her that far, she thought.

"Well," she said suddenly, her voice sounding very small and far away. "What lesson do you normally have at the beginning of the day?"

"Maths," said a boy in the front. "We do mathematics on Monday, Wednesday and Friday. On Tuesday and Thursday we do history."

Jenny thought quickly. At least she was quite good at mathematics – it was her strongest subject in fact. But would she be able to teach it? It was hard enough to be able to do complicated sums, but it must be even more difficult to teach other people how to do them.

"Get out your maths books, then," she said. "Start where you left off and do the whole page."

Desks were opened and the maths books were fished out. Then, with a busy murmur, the class got down to work. Jenny sat in her chair and looked about her. Perhaps I could dash out while they were all working, she thought. I could tell them that I was going to get something from the staff room, and run away once I was out of the door. Yes. That was the way to do it.

She rose to her feet.

"Carry on with your maths," she said, trying to sound as firm as possible. "I've just got to get something from the staff room."

"Please, miss," called out George Apple. "I'll go and fetch it for you."

"No," said Jenny. "You stay here and work. I'll just be a moment."

Not looking behind her, she walked across to the classroom door, opened it, and went out into the corridor. Nobody was about and so she started to walk purposefully towards the door at the far end.

She had got about half way when she heard footsteps. Somebody was coming round the corner and, in an awful moment of panic, Jenny realized that there was nowhere to hide. She would shortly come face to face with the person who was coming around the corner – whoever that might be.

Chapter Three

It turned out to be a rather severe-looking woman, a little bit taller than Jenny, wearing small round glasses and with very short, red hair. When she saw Jenny, she fixed her with a firm gaze and walked quickly towards her.

"So," she said. "You're the new teacher. I'm very glad to see you."

Jenny swallowed hard, wondering what to say.

"I'm Miss Ice, the Principal," said the woman. "And may I ask where you're

going? We normally don't leave our classrooms unattended at this school."

Jenny looked down at the ground. She was completely terrified of this severe-looking woman and, even if she knew what to say, she doubted whether her tongue would work.

"Well?" said the Principal. "Are you going back to the classroom?"

Jenny nodded miserably and, under the Principal's suspicious stare, she walked quickly back to her classroom.

Everybody was still working on their maths when Jenny got back. The classroom was quiet – rather unusually so, and Jenny wondered whether something was going on. Nobody was whispering to one another and every head was bent over a book. Jenny sat down at her table and looked down at the class. What was the reason for the quiet? Was the maths all that difficult? Surely not.

Suddenly she heard a noise. It was not a loud noise – more of a scuffling sound. She strained her ears to hear it better. It had gone, but then it came back – an odd, scraping sound, rather as if something was scraping at a bit of paper.

Jenny looked behind her. There was nothing there. She turned to face the class again, and she saw that several people were looking up at her. One of them was George Apple, and he was grinning broadly.

"Is there something wrong, miss?" he said.

Jenny shook her head.

"No," she said. "I thought I heard a noise, but I think it's gone."

Everybody looked up now, and Jenny noticed that most of the class was grinning. This was a trick of some kind – she was sure of it.

"I heard a noise too, miss," said George Apple. "I thought it was coming from the drawer in your desk."

Jenny looked down. The noise was there again, and yes, it did seem to be coming from the drawer.

"Why not open the drawer and take a look," suggested George Apple. "Just to check."

Jenny reached out and opened the drawer, and the moment she did so out jumped the largest brown rat she had ever seen. Jenny pushed her chair back as quickly as she could, letting out a

scream that made the windows rattle.

"A rat!" she shrieked. "A great big rat."

The rat had now landed on her table and was scurrying around, wondering what all the fuss was.

"You've got a rat on your table, miss," said George Apple, helpfully. "Should I take it away for you?"

Jenny nodded miserably. She had

always been scared of rats and when it had popped its head out of the drawer her heart had almost stopped. She sat quite still as George Apple sauntered up to her desk, picked up the rat by its tail, and took it back to his desk. Then he slipped it into his bag, and sat back at his desk.

Every eye was on Jenny. Some people were trying not to laugh, and succeeding. Others were giggling under their breath. Everybody thought it very funny – except Jenny. She had no idea what to do. Should she report George Apple to the Principal? If she did that, she would have to face Miss Ice again though, and that was the last thing she wanted to do. So she decided to get back to maths and to forget about rats for the time being.

"Will you give us the answers now?" asked one of the girls. "I hope I've got everything right!"

Jenny took the girl's book and looked at it. The work seemed rather difficult to her, and she was not sure if she would be able to do it.

"Well, let's see," she said. "I'll call out the answers and you can all mark your own work."

Reading out from the girl's book, she called out the answers.

"Problem number one – the answer is two thousand three hundred and forty-two."

Nobody said it wasn't, and so Jenny moved on to the next problem, and the problem after that. Each time she called out the answer she saw in the girl's exercise book, and each time, it seemed to her, she had the good luck to be quite correct.

"Thank you," she said to the girl as she handed her book back. "You're obviously very good at maths. Well done."

Now what? They had finished their mathematics, and Jenny did not fancy the idea of doing any more. She might not be so lucky this time, and it would be terrible not to be able to do the sums she was meant to be teaching.

An idea came to her.

"Let's do some geography," she said. "Can anybody tell me what the capital of France is?"

"That's easy," several voices called out. "Paris."

"Good," said Jenny. "Now what about Italy? Who knows the capital of Italy?"

Several hands went up, and Jenny pointed to a boy at the back.

"Cairo?" he said.

Everyone roared with laughter.

"That's in Egypt," said George Apple, in disgust. "Everyone knows it's Rome."

Jenny thought quickly. Perhaps she

should try something harder.

"What's the capital of . . ." she paused for a moment, trying to think of a country. "Yes, that's a good idea. What's the capital of Australia?"

The word Australia just slipped out, because Australia had somehow come to her mind. But no sooner had she said it, than she realized, with shock, that she had no idea at all what the capital of Australia was. There was a hope, of course, that somebody would know. If only somebody came out with the right answer, then she would not be shown up.

There was a silence. People looked at one another, and one or two scratched their heads. Then a girl in the middle row raised her hand slowly.

Jenny felt a surge of relief.

"Yes," she said. "You look as if you know the answer."

"Sydney," the girl said. Then she added: "I think."

Jenny had been very happy to hear Sydney, but was less pleased to hear the "I think" added on at the end.

Was Sydney the capital city of Australia? Surely it must be, now she came to think of it. It was so big and it had that great big bridge and that wonderful white opera house. When you thought of an Australian town you always thought of Sydney. It must be the capital.

"That's right," she said. "Well done. That was not an easy question."

She was about to ask another question, when she saw George Apple's hand go up.

"Yes, George," she said. "Do you have a question?"

"It's not Sydney," he said simply.

Jenny looked at him. Was he trying to be troublesome, or could he possibly be right?

"Of course it's Sydney," she said. "We all know it's Sydney, don't we everybody?"

"Yes," said a lot of voices. "Of course it's Sydney."

"It isn't," said George. "I've been there, and I know."

Suddenly everybody became quiet. Jenny stared at George Apple for a few moments. Had he really been there, she wondered, or was he just pretending?

"Well," she said after a while. "If

you're so clever and you've been there, you tell us what the right answer is."

"Canberra," said George simply. "Canberra's the capital of Australia. And look, I've got an atlas here to prove it."

Nobody said a word. The whole class stared at Jenny, who said nothing, but just stood there, becoming redder and redder.

Just at that moment, the door behind her opened and another teacher walked in.

"Is your class ready for gym?" she asked. "You're late already."

Jenny heaved a sigh of relief. Sydney, and Canberra, and even Australia itself could be forgotten now. Thank heavens for gym!

Chapter Four

The gymnasium was a large hall with a creaky wooden floor and all sorts of exciting equipment arranged around the walls. There were wooden horses for jumping over; ropes to swing on; and wooden bars for climbing up. Jenny was delighted. This was very much better than mathematics or geography. She could really teach gym, she thought, even if she wasn't a real teacher.

The pupils all changed into their gym outfits and stood waiting expectantly for Jenny's instructions.

"Can we play with the sand bags?" one of them asked.

"No," said another. "Can we get the trampoline out?"

Jenny clapped her hands, just as she remembered her last gym teacher doing. Everybody fell silent.

"We'll do some vaulting first," she said, in a firm, gym-teacher-type voice. "Make a long line and jump over the horse one by one."

The members of the class quickly fell into line and started to jump, one by one, over the wooden horse. Most of them did it quite well, although there were one or two who got stuck half way and had to be helped across.

After everybody had jumped over the horse twice, Jenny decided it was time for something a little bit more adventurous.

"We're going to climb the bars now," she said. "Everybody will climb right up to the top and then climb down again."

They started, one by one, to climb the bars. The first girl went up very quickly, and then shot down again in no time at all. The second was almost as fast, but not quite, but the third was best of all. She climbed up and down so quickly that you could hardly see her. Then it was George Apple's turn.

He was much slower, and clearly felt rather nervous over the whole thing. He took a lot of time to reach the top and then, when he did, he stopped.

"Come down now," Jenny called out. "The next person wants a turn."

George looked down at the floor of the gym and turned quite pale.

"I can't," he said, his voice shaky with fear. "I'm stuck."

"Come on," urged Jenny. "Just climb down the same way as you climbed up. It's simple."

George gulped and slowly lowered a foot to the rung below. There was a creaking noise and then the sound of snapping. Jenny caught her breath as a large section of the bars gave way beneath George. If he had not been properly stuck before, he certainly was now.

George let out a wail.

"I can't," he shouted out. "The bars have gone!"

Jenny dashed forward and looked up at George. He was right – he was absolutely stuck.

"He's going to die, miss," said George's best friend. "That's the end of him. So sad. Goodbye, George! Can I have your rat?"

"Oh, miss!" wailed one of the girls. "Poor George! He's not all that bad. It'll be an awful pity to lose him!'

Jenny looked about her. She was the teacher, and she would have to save George. But how?

Her gaze fell on the ropes tied up against the opposite wall. Yes, that was the way to do it! She could use the ropes. It was exactly what Tarzan would do, if he were there.

Wasting no time, Jenny ran to the other side of the gym and untied the thickest rope. Then she tucked her skirt up, climbed a short distance up the rope, and pushed herself away from the wall with all her vigour.

Like the pendulum of a great clock, the rope, with Jenny clinging to it, swung all the way across the gym. There was a gasp from the pupils as Jenny sailed her way across the void, and a sigh as her outstretched hand narrowly missed the terrified George. But Jenny was not put off by failure, and when she swung back to the other side she pushed herself off again with all the strength she could muster.

This time she reached George with no difficulty, and, taking him quite by surprise, wrenched him off the bars with one hand. Then, holding on to him with all her strength, she sailed back on the rope to the other side and then slid down to the ground, George and all.

As her feet touched the floorboards, a great cheer arose from the class.

"Well done!" they shouted. "Well done! You've saved George's life!"

George stood up on his rather shaky legs and dusted himself down.

"Thank you," he said to Jenny. "I'll never forget that. You're a real heroine, miss!"

"Oh, it was nothing," said Jenny, casually. "That's what teachers are for, aren't they?"

George looked down at the floor. He was clearly feeling ashamed of himself.

"Sorry about the rat, miss," he said. 'I was just having a bit of fun."

Jenny smiled. "Don't worry about that," she said. "It *was* quite a good joke, I suppose."

Everybody was too excited after that to do much more gym, and so they all changed back into their ordinary clothes and began to go back to the classroom. Jenny told them to go in twos, with each person having a partner, and for some reason this seemed to please everybody.

On the way, they saw the Principal, or rather, she saw them. She was standing in the doorway to the library as they went past, and she frowned crossly as Jenny walked by.

"What a horrible person," thought Jenny. "She's obviously very cross about something. I wonder what it can be?"

Chapter Five

Jenny was soon to find out why Miss Ice had looked so cross. Just as the class reached their desks again, with everybody talking in an excited way about how George had been rescued by the new teacher, the bell went for break.

As she had promised, Alison, the teacher who had been so friendly earlier on, came back to show Jenny to the staff room. Jenny had to give up any thought of running away now – it would have been very rude to Alison to do that.

She was very worried about going into the staff room, because she thought that she was bound to be found out there. But Alison was very helpful and poured out a cup of tea for her, also giving her first choice of biscuits. Then Jenny sat down, with Alison at her side, and began to drink her tea.

The other teachers were all looking at her, and Jenny felt very awkward about it. But they all seemed quite friendly too, and Jenny soon relaxed.

But not for long.

"Where were you teaching before you came here?" asked one of the other teachers politely.

Jenny had been about to take a sip of her tea, but her hand froze halfway to her lips.

"Er . . ." she began. "Where was I a teacher?"

"That's what I asked," said the other teacher.

Everybody looked expectantly at Jenny, but her mind was a complete blank. Then a place came into her mind, and she blurted it out, relieved that at least she could give some answer.

"Canberra," she said.

"Oh!" exclaimed one of the other teachers. "How interesting. Please tell us all about it."

Jenny felt her cheeks burning red.

"It's in Australia," she said.

Everybody laughed.

"Oh, we know that," said somebody. "But what's it like?"

Jenny looked at the floor. This was terrible. Why had she not run away on the way to the staff room? At least then she would have been spared this terrible nightmare.

"It's very nice there," she said. "What with the sea and everything."

There was a silence. Then one of the teachers sitting at the far end of the room said something.

"Sea?" he snorted. "Canberra's hundreds of miles from the sea."

Jenny looked at him.

"I didn't say it wasn't," she said defiantly.

"But you did," he said. "You said the sea was what made Canberra a nice place."

Jenny shook her head.

"That's not what I meant," she said, trying to sound slightly cross. "I meant that if you don't like the sea, and you want to be far away from it, then Canberra's a good place to be."

A few of the teachers looked a bit puzzled by this, but, to Jenny's great relief, it was at this moment that the Principal came in and everybody turned in her direction. She did not look very happy, and Jenny noticed that for some reason the Principal was glaring straight at her.

Jenny's heart sank.

"She must know," she said to herself. "She must have found out!"

The Principal helped herself to a cup of tea. Then she examined the plate of biscuits, took the largest, most chocolatey one left, and bit into it with a resounding crunch. As she did so, she shot a furious glance at Jenny.

"I saw your class going back after gym," the Principal said frostily. "I noticed that they were walking in pairs."

Jenny looked about her for support, but everybody was looking at the Principal.

"Yes," she said after a while. "I think they were."

The Principal swallowed the last of her biscuit and cleared her throat.

"In this school," she said, her voice still cool, "the pupils always walk single file. That's the way we do it."

"But that's silly!" Jenny blurted out. "That means that they must take twice as long to go anywhere."

As Jenny spoke, some of the other teachers drew in their breath loudly. They seemed to be shocked that anybody was daring to tell the Principal that she was wrong and they were watching closely to see what would happen next.

The Principal put down her teacup with shaking hands.

"I beg your pardon?" she said. "Did I hear you correctly? Did you say it's actually better to let the pupils walk in pairs? Is that what you're saying?"

Jenny shrugged her shoulders.

"Yes," she said simply. "That's right. After all, it does seem more sensible, doesn't it?"

The Principal let out a sound which was half a snort and half a puff of rage.

"That's not the point," she hissed

between clenched teeth. "If I say something is to be done a certain way, then that's the way it is to be done!"

"But what if it's better to do it another way?" said Jenny, feeling and sounding very miserable. "Surely you should do something the best way rather than do it another way just because that's the way it's always been done."

The Principal stared at Jenny, her mouth open in astonishment that anybody would actually dare to talk like this.

Then, from the other side of the room, one of the other teachers spoke out.

"She's right," he said. "I don't see why we should always do things the way they've been done in the past. And anyway, why don't we vote on it?"

"Good idea," said another teacher.

"Yes," said another. "Let's vote."

So the teachers all voted, and everybody, except for the Principal, voted to allow the pupils to walk from classroom to classroom in twos, or even threes. The Principal was dumbstruck and, after she had finished her tea, she slunk out of the room, looking quite confused and unhappy.

"Thank you," whispered one of the teachers sitting next to Jenny. "You've done what we've all been itching to do for years. You've put Miss Ice in her place! Well done!"

"Let's all celebrate by having another chocolate biscuit," said Alison, reaching for the biscuit plate.

"But Miss Ice said we can only have one a day," said somebody else.

"I don't care," said Alison. "In fact, I'm going to have three!"

All the other teachers agreed, and as they sat around finishing off every chocolate biscuit on the plate, they smiled warmly at Jenny.

"You haven't been here a full day," said somebody. "And already you've changed things for the better."

Jenny didn't know what to reply. She had not meant to offend the Principal like that and she hoped that everybody, including Miss Ice, would forget about it as soon as possible. All that she wanted now was to get home and to ask her parents to come to the school to sort out the mistake. But there were still

several lessons left to be taught and so
she would have to survive those before
she could get away. Would it be easy?
She had a dreadful feeling it would not.

Chapter Six

The bell went and everyone returned to their classrooms. Jenny found all the pupils in her class already in their seats, looking at her expectantly. They had been most impressed by her rescue of George Apple, and they wondered what this exciting new teacher would have in store for them next.

It was chemistry. Jenny had not planned to have a chemistry lesson – she had not planned to have any lesson, in fact – but when she saw the box marked

Chemistry she thought it would be a good idea.

Everybody agreed. They watched carefully as she placed the box on her desk and took out the various bowls and bottles inside. There were also jars of chemical powders – red powders, white powders, blue powders – and these she put neatly to one side.

"I shall now teach you some chemistry," she said to the class.

Picking up a jar of white powder, she opened it and peered at it carefully. The powder looked a little bit like sugar, but it smelled quite different. In fact, it smelled a bit like rotten eggs.

"I'm going to mix a bit of this powder with the red powder," Jenny explained. "Then we'll add a bit of the blue powder, just to be on the safe side."

"Why?" called out a boy from the back. "Why are you mixing the powders together?"

Jenny looked at him scornfully.

"Because that's what chemistry is all about," she replied. "And anyway, have you got any better ideas?"

The boy shook his head.

"Well, then," Jenny went on. "Here goes!"

She poured some of the white powder into a dish and then, standing well back, poured a small quantity of red powder in and mixed them up. Nothing happened.

"You've got to put in much more, miss," said one of the girls at the front. "Our last teacher used to put in loads and loads of powder."

"I know," said Jenny crossly. "I'm just testing it to see if it works. I'm going to add much more now."

She took up the jar and tipped the rest of the red powder into the mixture. Then she stirred it a little with a long glass rod.

Something was happening now. The mixture was beginning to sizzle a bit. Jenny stood a bit further back. You never knew with chemistry – odd things could happen.

And they did. Suddenly there was a puff of smoke and a bang. Jenny gave a start, and a few people let out whistles of surprise. A cloud of green smoke was now rising up from the dish and beginning to fill that corner of the room.

"There," said Jenny triumphantly. "You see, that's chemistry. It works."

The cloud of smoke seemed to be getting bigger and bigger, and every now and then it made a rather strange, popping sound. It was really rather alarming, thought Jenny, but at least it could not go on for ever. Sooner or later the chemicals would calm down and the cloud of thick green smoke would disappear.

It was while Jenny was thinking this that the door of the classroom opened. Jenny turned round to see Miss Ice standing in the doorway, a look of anger and outrage on her face.

"What is happening here?" the Principal demanded. "What is the meaning of this . . . this green cloud?"

"Chemistry," called out one of the boys.

"Silence!" hissed the Principal. "Miss
. . . Miss whatever your name is, what
do you think you're doing filling the
classroom with green smoke?"

She did not wait for an answer.
Striding forward, she went straight into
the middle of the cloud of green smoke,
waving at it with her arms.

"I shall put a stop to this," she
spluttered. "I have never seen anything
as disgraceful in my . . ."

Her voice broke off. The Principal
had disappeared into the swirling cloud
of smoke and now there was not a single
sign of her.

"She's dissolved!" shouted George
Apple. "Miss, you've dissolved the
Principal!"

"Oh dear," thought Jenny. "I really
shouldn't have tried chemistry. If only
I'd stuck to geography."

Suddenly there was a coughing sound

and the Principal reappeared from the cloud, holding the dish of chemicals, which she had now covered with a cloth.

"This is a disgrace!" she stormed. "You could have blown us all up!"

Jenny was about to say how sorry she was, but stopped. There was something funny about the Principal, and all the class noticed it too. Her hair, which had been red when she came into the room, was now quite green!

"Excuse me," Jenny said. "I'm very sorry, but your hair . . ."

"Don't you talk about my hair," said the Principal. "There's nothing wrong with my hair. You just open all these windows and get the smoke out of the classroom."

Jenny did as she was asked, but as she did so everybody else started laughing. They had tried to conceal their mirth over the Principal's funny hair, but it was just too difficult. Soon everybody was holding their sides, the tears of laughter streaming down their faces.

Miss Ice stormed out of the classroom, holding the dish of chemicals in her hand. But just before she left, she stopped and turned in Jenny's direction.

"You're dismissed!" she said. "You will leave the school immediately!"

The laughter stopped. Now everybody sat as quiet as mice, looking at Jenny.

"That's not fair!" said George Apple. "You saved my life!"

"You're the best teacher we've ever had," said another. "Please don't go."

Jenny felt touched by these kind remarks, but at the same time she felt very pleased that she had been sacked. Her being a teacher could not last, and she was relieved that it was all over.

But before she went, she thought she
would do one last thing.

"Let's have a picnic," she said. "It's
far too nice a day to sit inside and do
lessons."

Chapter Seven

Out into the school garden they all trooped, taking with them the sandwiches they were meant to have for lunch. They found a good place, and they all sat, enjoying the sunshine and munching sandwiches and crisps. Everybody was very happy.

Jenny sat next to a girl called Lucy, who told her how much she had enjoyed the school day.

"Our last teacher was very nice," said Lucy. "But not nearly as much fun as you are."

Jenny smiled and thanked Lucy. Then Lucy took two lollipops out of her pocket and offered one to Jenny. Jenny was very pleased. Lollipops were her favourite sweet, and red lollipops were her favourite of favourites.

And that is what she was doing, sucking a red lollipop, when the Principal stormed out of the building, her green hair waving in the breeze, and came over to stand indignantly in front of Jenny.

The Principal looked down at Jenny, her mouth wide open in astonishment.

"I can't believe my eyes,' she said at last. "I never thought I'd see the day when a teacher – a teacher, mind you – would be sitting out in the school garden sucking a lollipop!"

Jenny took the lollipop out of her mouth and was about to say how sorry she was. But she had no chance to say anything, as just at that moment the school secretary came running across the grass.

"There's a telephone call for you," she said to the Principal. "And it's urgent."

The Principal gave Jenny a withering look, and turned on her heels. Then, together with the school secretary, she strode off in the direction of the office.

The telephone call turned out to be a very strange conversation indeed.

"I'm so sorry about not being there today," said a voice at the other end of the line. "I seem to have put the wrong day in my diary. I thought I was starting tomorrow."

Miss Ice frowned in annoyance.

"I have no idea what you're talking about," she snapped at the caller. "Where are you? And why do you think you should be here, rather than there? And *who* are you, anyway?"

"I was meant to be there today," said

75

the voice. "I thought today was tomorrow. I mean I thought that tomorrow was today. I thought that . . ."

"But why do you think you have to be here tomorrow, or today?" said the Principal in a voice that was by now becoming extremely vexed.

"Because I told you that I was going to be here, or rather there, today. I mean, that today was when I was going to start, rather than tomorrow."

The Principal drew in her breath.

"Let's start at the beginning," she said coldly. "Who are you?"

"I'm your new teacher, of course," said the voice. "I was meant to be starting today."

"But you have," said Miss Ice. "You're here."

"No I'm not," said the voice. "I'm not there. I'm here. And that's the problem."

"But I've just seen the new teacher," protested Miss Ice. "I've just been talking to her. She was sucking a lollipop . . ."

"A lollipop?" asked the voice at the other end, sounding very surprised. "I don't eat lollipops. I used to, of course, but that was a long time ago. Chocolates, yes, that's a different matter . . ."

Miss Ice cut her short. It was now becoming clear to her that there was something very strange happening.

"Very well," she said in her steeliest voice. "Very well. You don't eat lollipops and you're not here. Just come along as soon as you can."

And with that she put down the receiver and stormed out of the office.

Jenny was still sitting with her friends when Miss Ice returned. They had not noticed the Principal return and they all

got a shock when they heard the angry
voice bellowing out behind them.

"Now I know," cried the Principal,
her voice cracking with anger. "You're
not a teacher at all!" She paused.
"You're a . . . you're a girl!"

Jenny dropped her lollipop. She could
not deny it. It was all over.

"It wasn't my fault," she said. "I
didn't want to be a teacher at all. I didn't
start it . . ."

The Principal, who was now quivering with rage, took a step forward, and stood on the lollipop. She looked down at her right shoe, which now had a lollipop stuck to it. Then she bent down to scrape off the sticky mess, and that was Jenny's chance.

"Run!" whispered Lucy. "Quick!"

Jenny leapt to her feet and ran across the garden towards the school gate. The Principal started to give chase, but Jenny was far too quick for her and had soon disappeared round the corner. She had made it!

After a while, Jenny stopped running and began to walk. She looked over her shoulder to see whether she was still being chased, but there was no sign of anybody following her. She breathed a sigh of relief and turned the corner into her own street.

As she did so, she almost bumped into a woman who was walking in the opposite direction.

"I'm sorry," said the woman, looking anxiously at her watch. "I wasn't really looking where I was going." She paused. "Could you help me? I'm very late, and very lost."

"Of course," said Jenny. "Where are you going?"

"Well," said the woman. "It's rather a long story. I put the wrong date in my diary. I thought today was tomorrow, or the other way round, I'm not sure. I'm trying to find the school near here. Street Pond School. I'm the new teacher

there and I'm terribly late. I've just been
speaking to the Principal on the
telephone, Miss Frost I think she's
called. And she sounded terribly hot, I
mean cold, about it all."

Jenny listened to this carefully, and as
she did so she began to smile. This was
the real teacher, the teacher whose place
she had taken for the day.

"You're not far away," she said. "If
you walk down that road, turn left, and

then carry on all the way up the street you'll reach the school."

"Thank you," said the woman gratefully. "I do hope that my class has been looked after this morning."

"Oh I think they had quite an interesting morning," Jenny said. "They studied rats, I mean maths. And then they did gym. I shouldn't worry about that if I were you."

The real teacher thanked her and went off on her way. Jenny watched her as she went, pleased that they had bumped into one another. She liked the sound of the new teacher and she was sure that the pupils would too.

But Jenny had not yet solved all her problems. Although she had managed to get away from the school, she would have to go back there the next day. And what would happen then? How could you go back to a school where you had dyed the Principal's hair green? Miss Ice would not forget something like that in a hurry.

Jenny was thinking of this, feeling quite miserable, as she walked in the front door of her house. So she paid very little attention to her mother's calling her until her mother rushed out of the sitting room and gave her a big hug.

"There you are!" her mother said. "What a relief! I've been so worried about you! Where were you?"

"At school," said Jenny simply.

"But the school telephoned," said her mother. "They said that you hadn't arrived this morning. You can imagine how worried I was!"

Jenny sat down and sunk her head in her hands. It was going to be very difficult to explain.

"I *was* at school," she said. "Or rather, I went to school. But there was an awful mistake, you see. They thought I was a teacher."

Her mother looked at her in astonishment.

"Do you mean they put you in charge of a class?" she exclaimed.

Jenny nodded.

"It was terrible to start with," she said. "But then it got better. In fact, I think that all the children enjoyed themselves very much."

"I see," said her mother. "Well, I shall be able to phone Mr Brown now and tell him not to worry."

Jenny was puzzled.

"Mr Brown?"

"The Principal of Pond Street School," said her mother. "I spoke to him on the phone this morning. He was very puzzled as to why you weren't there."

"But the Principal isn't Mr Brown," protested Jenny. "It's Miss Ice. She's a lady with green . . . I mean, red hair."

Jenny's mother looked surprised. Then a smile spread slowly over her face as she realized what had happened.

"Jenny," she explained, her voice breaking into a laugh. "You went to Street Pond School, didn't you? That's the other school! You were due to go to Pond Street School."

Jenny began to laugh too.

"So I don't have to go back there," she said. "What a relief!"

She was very pleased that she would not have to face the Principal again. She was also pleased that she would not have had to explain to all her pupils at the school that she may have started off as a teacher but was coming back as a girl. That would have seemed very odd to everybody.

So she went to school the next day – to the right school this time – and she was very happy there. She didn't have to sit at the teacher's desk and she did not have to conduct any lessons. It was wonderful to be able to sit there, not having to know the answers to everything.

And as for Street Pond School, well her day there had changed things in more ways than one. A few weeks later, while she was helping her mother with her shopping, she met Alison, the friendly teacher, in the supermarket.

"There you are!" exclaimed Alison. "I'm really glad that I saw you. I wanted to thank you for making things so much better at the school."

Jenny was puzzled, but Alison explained everything to her.

"You see, after what happened in the staff room, we all decided that we would stand up to Miss Ice and not let her push us around quite so much. So we started to vote on all the important things. And since there were far more of us than of

the Principal, the school began to be run
the way we had always wanted."

"I'm glad," said Jenny. "I thought
that I had just caused trouble that day."

"Not at all," said Alison, smiling.
"And another thing – Miss Ice got used
to the new way of doing things and
became far, far less bossy. She's really
quite nice now!"

"I'm very pleased," said Jenny.

"But the oddest thing of all," said
the teacher, "is what happened about

Miss Ice's hair. She decided that she rather liked her hair the colour you made it – green. So now she has it dyed green permanently, and it suits her very well!"

"So everybody's happy?" asked Jenny.

"Yes," said the teacher. "Everybody is very happy. What's more, any time you'd like to come back as a teacher for a day or so, please do!"

Jenny thanked her warmly. She did not think that she would go back, but it was nice to know that the invitation was there. She thought back on her day as a teacher. She hadn't done so badly after all. She had sorted out George Apple, and saved his life as well. She had stood up to Miss Ice, and made her much better while she was about it. And she had given the whole class something to laugh about. Perhaps she would go back now and then, just to make sure that things were still going well. After all, she thought, I was really quite good at it!

THE END

CALCULATOR ANNIE
Alexander McCall Smith

'You're a genius!'

Annie, who has always been hopeless at even the simplest sums, wakes up one morning to discover she has turned into a mathematical genius. To everyone's amazement, she can now do the most difficult calculations in the world – and in a few seconds, too! Annie finds herself helping out at the bank and at the local newspaper, and even gets entered for a competition. But will her extraordinary talent last?

0 552 526649

YOUNG CORGI

MIKE'S MAGIC SEEDS
Alexander McCall Smith

A horrid shopkeeper tricks Mike out of
the last of his pocket money for a strange
packet of seeds . . . which grow into the
most amazing plants! Each one produces
a different kind of sweet – marzipan,
chocolate flake, sugar almonds and more.
Taking some pieces to school makes him
extremely popular with everyone – except
his old friend Tim.

Then nosy Angela starts asking awkward
questions. If Mike isn't careful, she might
discover his secret and ruin everything . . .

0 552 52476X

THE GUARD DOG
Dick King-Smith

'Out of his hairy little mouth came the most awful noise you can possibly imagine . . .'

There are six puppies in the pet shop window; five posh pedigree puppies, and a scruffy little mongrel with a grand ambition – to be a guard dog.

The other pups laugh at him. How can such a small, scruffy dog possibly expect to be bought to guard a home? Especially when his bark is the most horrible, ear-splitting racket they have ever heard! Will the poor little guard dog be doomed to a lonely life in the Dogs' Home – or worse . . . ?

0 552 527319

THE OLDEST SNOWMAN IN THE WORLD
Eric Johns

'Warm weather,' Mr Crystal announced. 'I can feel it in the breeze. It will soon be the melting time.'

Amanda and Timmy can't bear the thought of losing their wonderful snowman. He may be a strange shape, and he may be a bit grumpy at times, but Mr Crystal is without doubt the best snowman ever.

But Mr Crystal, like all snowmen, is doomed. As the warmer weather approaches fast, the children know they must come up with a plan to save their friend. Somehow they must help Mr Crystal to live on through the spring and summer – and to become the oldest snowman in the world.

0 552 527491

E114532

SINK OR SWIM
Ghillian Potts

'IT WAS AN ACCIDENT!'

Every Tuesday, William goes to the swimming baths with the rest of his class. But no-one knows if William can swim properly or not, for he always stays close to the side, frightened of being ducked. Big Mark, the class nuisance, knows this – but it doesn't stop him jumping in right on top of William, pushing him underwater!

No-one believes Big Mark when he says it was an accident. For Big Mark is *always* rushing around, banging into even the smallest children and knocking them over. Then William has an idea – a way of making Big Mark stop. But as William's plan begins to work, he and Big Mark are thrown together in a dramatic adventure – an adventure in which William *must* overcome his fear of the water . . .

0 552 52753X

YOUNG CORGI